DROUGHT AND HEAT WAVES

A PRACTICAL SURVIVAL GUIDE

Natalie Goldstein

rosen
central™

The Rosen Publishing Group, Inc., New York

Published in 2006 by The Rosen Publishing Group, Inc.
29 East 21st Street, New York, NY 10010

First Edition

Library of Congress Cataloging-in-Publication Data

Goldstein, Natalie.
Drought and heat waves: a practical survival guide / Natalie Goldstein.
      p. cm.—(The library of emergency preparedness)
Includes bibliographical references.
ISBN 1-4042-0536-5 (library binding)
1. Droughts—Juvenile literature. 2. Heat waves (Meteorology)—Juvenile literature. 3. Emergency management—United States—Juvenile literature. I. Title. II. Series.
QC929.25.G65 2005
363.34'929–dc22

2005016221

Manufactured in Malaysia

On the cover: A pond that gets its water from the Columbia River in Washington State shows the effects of drought.

CONTENTS

Introduction

It was the worst drought and heat wave to hit Europe in more than 150 years. Heavy rains that had developed in West Africa in late July 2003 pushed a weather system over North Africa that funneled hot air from the Sahara Desert. This system then moved over western Europe. It remained there most of the month of August, blocking the cooling, rain-bearing clouds that form over the Atlantic Ocean from moving over the region. Temperatures climbed above 100 degrees Fahrenheit (38 degrees Celsius). On August 12, Paris reached a record high of 104°F (40°C).

In France alone, 14,000 people would die in the resulting heat wave. These were predominantly elderly people who lived alone. They lacked resources such as air-conditioning or fans to cool themselves.

Fires swept from Spain to Sweden. Some were sparked by lightning, while others were sparked by people starting campfires and barbeques, or carelessly dropping lit cigarettes to the ground. Firefighters fought the blazes, but numerous lives were lost before people could be evacuated. The heat caused several train tracks to buckle. Trains across Europe ran cautiously at slower speeds. Highways were also in danger of buckling in the extreme heat, causing heavy traffic as cars crept along. In the United Kingdom, police and other state officials handed out water to trapped motorists. Several young people drowned when seeking relief from the heat in treacherous bodies of water. In Germany, the levels of the Danube and Rhine rivers, both major transportation routes, dropped so low that they became barely navigable channels, putting freight ships in danger of running aground. Farmers lost crops, making the price of fresh fruit and vegetables rise for the consumer. In Paris, residents without air conditioners or fans sought shelter under the Eiffel Tower. Tourists bathed themselves in the fountains at the Louvre museum.

One of the most recent heat wave disasters to hit the United States took place for a week in July 1995, in Chicago, Illinois. It began on July 12. By July 13, with the combined

People cool themselves in the Trocadero fountain near the Eiffel Tower during the massive heat wave on August 9, 2003, in Paris, France. For the most part, people in France were unaccustomed to such extreme heat and as a result were unprepared. Also, many people went on vacation in the month of August, and they were not present to check in on vulnerable loved ones who had underestimated the heat.

heat and humidity making the temperature feel like it was 120°F (49°C), heat-related effects began to take their toll on the city's residents. People without air conditioners in their homes ran fans and opened windows. Yet this action only recirculated hot air. Those who did have air conditioners began to overload the power grid. This extensive demand for electricity led to loss of power in some neighborhoods. In those same areas, people opened fire hydrants in an effort to get to water and cool off, causing a loss of water pressure in addition to the power loss. Children

became dehydrated and nauseous. Firefighters had to hose them down. City roads buckled in the heat. People began to be hospitalized for heat-related illnesses. Soon the hospitals were at capacity and turned people away. Other people never made it to the hospital, causing the death toll to rise to record numbers for Chicago: a total of 465 deaths were considered heat related. For the week of July 13 to 21, the number of deaths totaled 1,177. For that same period of time in 1994, there were only 637 deaths.

An exhausted Chicago, Illinois, policeman rests during the heat wave in July 1995. Most of the hundreds of victims of the heat wave lived in the heart of the city and did not have air-conditioning.

In the United States, heat waves (usually accompanied by drought) are the largest weather-related killer, often because people are not properly informed and prepared. In urban areas, due to fear of crime, people may not open windows for proper ventilation. People may not have fans or air conditioners.

In the following chapters, we will learn about drought and heat waves. We will list actions you should take to prepare yourself and your family should they strike. By being properly prepared, you can protect yourself and family members. You can be helpful by checking on vulnerable neighbors, such as young children or elderly people. There are also actions you can take that will contribute toward avoiding these types of disasters, which environmental experts predict will become more prevalent in the future.

1 --- What About Drought?

A drought is an extended period when rainfall amounts are significantly below normal. The period of below-normal rainfall usually must last for a minimum of several months, or one season or more. Often, however, droughts last for years.

The effects of a drought may be catastrophic, and people understandably think of droughts as natural disasters. Yet droughts are not rare or random events. Droughts occur as part of natural climate cycles—they are inevitable and occur periodically in many parts of the world.

Because a drought is a period of below-normal rainfall, or precipitation, it is defined differently in different regions. For example, the state of Maine generally gets about 40 inches (101.6 centimeters) of precipitation per year. In 2000, only about 25 inches (63.5 cm) of rain fell in Maine. In that year, Maine experienced a drought. Yet 25 inches of rain in Arizona is almost unheard of. It would probably cause floods! Arizona gets, on average, about 12 inches (30.5 cm) of rain per year. A drought in Arizona, such as the one that occurred in 1955, happens when this desert state gets far less than 10 inches (25.4 cm) of annual rainfall. In each case, drought is defined by the reduction in the average amount of rainfall that the region normally gets.

Types of Drought

Droughts are sometimes described based on their impacts. Agricultural droughts affect farmers and kill crops. Hydrological droughts lower water levels in rivers and lakes, and in groundwater. Meteorological droughts are defined by the degree of dryness of the climate compared to a long-term norm (this is the type of drought that varies from region to region, as between Maine and Arizona). Sometimes droughts are classified by the extent of social and economic damage they do. In these cases, the severity of the drought is related to the difference between the available supply of water during a drought and the human demand for the dwindling supplies of that water.

Droughts are sometimes classified by type based on how long they last and how severe they are. A seasonal drought happens in a region where most rainfall occurs during one rainy season. India, for example, gets most of its rain during the seasonal monsoon. If monsoon rains fail to show up, India experiences a seasonal drought. A devastating drought is one that is hard to predict and occurs without warning. An invisible drought occurs when evaporation exceeds rainfall. Groundwater levels fall, and water levels in lakes and rivers decline. It's hard to persuade people to save water during an invisible drought because there is some rainfall—just not enough to exceed the evaporation caused by high temperatures.

The Causes of Drought

Nearly all droughts are caused by changes in the patterns and movement of winds, which carry rain-giving clouds. Rain, of course, comes from clouds. Generally, clouds form when wind forces air to move upward. When wind forces air to move downward, clouds disappear. And so does the rain.

The west-to-east flow of winds at mid-latitudes such as North America brings what we think of as normal weather. In spring, as polar air moves north, winds flow in a more north-south direction. Occasionally, this change in direction makes wind patterns unstable. The unstable winds begin to circle in on themselves, forming high-pressure, circular cells. Sometimes, these high-pressure cells remain stationary over

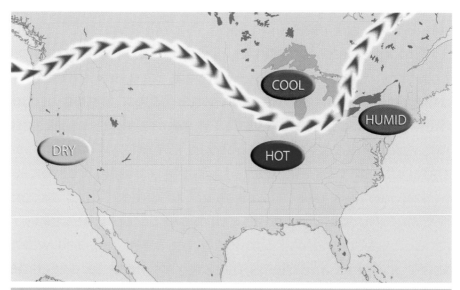

This is an illustration of the jet stream moving across the United States and Canada on what might be a typical summer day. This river of air made up of fast winds surrounding a core of slower winds directs storms and areas of high and low pressure. It is located about 20,000 feet (6,096 meters) above Earth.

a region for a long time, forming a blocking high. A blocking high causes a sinking, downward flow of air that prevents cloud formation. A blocking high is also an obstacle to cool, moisture-laden air, which flows around it. The land beneath the blocking high thus gets no clouds and no rain. If the blocking high stays put for too long, a drought may result.

In North America, winds flow from west to east on the jet stream, a large river of air several miles above the surface of Earth. In normal years, warm, moist air from the Caribbean moves north and joins the jet stream. When the westerly winds are blowing with their usual force, they absorb the southern winds and carry them eastward. On this journey, the warm air cools, clouds form, and rain falls as the air mass moves across the continent. During some years, conditions in the ocean and atmosphere change, blocking highs form, and drought results.

Predicting Drought

It is incredibly hard to predict most droughts. Weather is the result of complex interactions between the oceans and the atmosphere, and the conditions in each are widely vari-able. Scientists continuously monitor these conditions to detect the slightest changes that might affect the weather. Yet there are many variables that affect these two huge sys-tems. It is very difficult to predict a drought that is a month or more in the future. Changes in air and sea surface tem-perature and significant changes in precipitation patterns may signal the coming of drought. The amount of moisture in the soil, the type of land surface, and other factors affect how long a drought may last and how severe it will be.

☀ The Making of the Dust Bowl ☀

The drought that struck the Midwest in the 1930s was perhaps the greatest natural disaster the United States has ever experienced. The Great Plains, which include parts of Texas, Kansas, Oklahoma, Colorado, and New Mexico, came to be known as the Dust Bowl.

The Dust Bowl was the result of natural climate cycles made worse by human activity. Homesteaders first settled the Great Plains in the late 1800s. At that time, the region was experiencing a period of unusually wet weather. The farmers plowed the native prairie grasses. They planted water-hungry, shallow-rooted corn, wheat, and other crops. At first, crop yields were high because of the plentiful rains. But by the 1930s, the climate became drier. In fact, it became even drier than normal. The thirsty crops withered and died. The drought-tolerant prairie grasses that had held the soil in place with their deep root systems were long gone, destroyed by the farmers' plows. There was nothing growing on the land to hold the bone-dry soil. The strong winds that blew over the flat prairies lifted the dusty soil high into the air. They carried it in huge clouds that blanketed whole towns and farms under dust. Many millions of tons of once-rich topsoil simply blew away.

Thousands of farmers lost their farms and their livelihoods in the Dust Bowl. Their suffering stemmed from three factors that worked against them. First, they believed the abundant rains of the early settlement years were normal, and they planted water-loving crops accordingly. Second, they did not understand the prairie and how important it was to have drought-tolerant, soil-holding plants growing there. Third, when the years of unusually high rainfall ended, the climate did not slip into its pattern of normal rainfall. Instead, it crashed immediately into a severe drought. During the 1930s, rainfall on the Great Plains was 60 percent lower than normal.

This dramatic photograph taken in Boise City, Oklahoma, in 1935 shows the dust cloud rolling along the prairie after wind lifted the top layer of bone-dry soil from the ground. The dust storms lasted from 1930 to 1941. Witnesses described the thunderous roar of the clouds as they rolled through, dumping a layer of silt everywhere. Families stayed indoors, covering their faces with handkerchiefs.

El Niño and Drought

El Niño ("little boy" in Spanish) refers to abnormal conditions in the tropical Pacific Ocean that occur, on average, every three to seven years. During El Niño, air-pressure masses over the tropical Pacific reverse. This periodic "flip" is known as the Southern Oscillation, and the event is officially called the El Niño-Southern Oscillation, or ENSO. During ENSO, high-pressure air masses that normally occur in the eastern Pacific shift to the western Pacific, and low-pressure air masses that occur in the western Pacific flip over to the eastern Pacific.

During ENSO, the rain-producing warm-water pool that normally occurs in the western Pacific shifts eastward to the central Pacific. This shift has dramatic effects on wind patterns and rainfall around the globe. This shift has been associated with floods, severe storms, and droughts in many parts of the world. Scientists know that ENSO causes drought in Australia, Indonesia, and the Philippines. These places lie near the normal location of the warm-water pool in the Pacific. When the rain-generating warm-water pool moves eastward, it takes the rain with it, and these regions experience drought. ENSO also brings drought to India (it causes the monsoons to fail) and to Central and South America. Brazil's Amazon rain forest becomes tinder dry and may burn for months. In North America, ENSO causes a high-pressure cell to form in the northern Pacific. This blocking high plants itself over the Northwest and channels moisture-rich air masses around it. The Southeast may get lots of rain, but the Northwest, Midwest, and Northeast may experience drought.

El Niño brought severe drought conditions to the Amazon rain forest in 1998. Here, a fire burns in northern Brazil on March 16, 1998. More than 1,480,000 acres (600,000 hectares) of forest burned in the drought.

The Tropical Atmosphere Ocean (TAO) Project array is a series of equipment-laden buoys deployed along the equatorial Pacific. The buoys

A National Oceanic and Atmospheric Administration (NOAA) worker makes adjustments on a buoy that is part of the equatorial El Niño array. Seventy buoys make up the array from Papua, New Guinea, to the Galápagos Islands.

constantly monitor ocean and atmospheric conditions, and they are the most efficient means of predicting the onset of ENSO and the droughts that accompany it.

Droughts often occur without an ENSO event. In the United States, scientists and agricultural experts use different indexes to determine if a state or region is on its way to experiencing a full-blown drought. The Palmer Index, for example, monitors many variables, including precipitation and soil moisture content, to help predict if a severe drought is imminent. U.S. government agencies use the Palmer Index to determine when drought relief may be needed in any part of the country.

2 ... Preparing for a Drought

Drought is not like other natural disasters, such as tornadoes or earthquakes. These events occur suddenly, almost always without warning. More important, they don't last very long. In one way, though, droughts are similar to hurricanes in that both are sometimes predicted in advance. Yet a hurricane, no matter how destructive, blows by in a matter of days. Drought, on the other hand, lasts a long time. Its effects on people get worse as the drought continues. Planning for and coping with drought is different in many ways from emergency planning for hurricanes or other short-term disasters.

Water for Drinking

Storing water should be a part of any emergency plan. If you live in a drought-prone area, or if a drought is predicted for your region, a large supply of clean, bottled water is essential. People need to drink about eight cups of water a day to remain healthy. That's about 1 quart (0.9 liter) of water per day per person. Try to keep enough bottled water on hand for everyone in your family for at least one to two weeks. (And don't forget your pets!) Remember, though, that bottled water—like any other bottled liquid—is usable for only a limited amount of time. If you buy bottled water, look on the bottles for a "use-by" date. Even if there is no

Various brands of bottled water are displayed here. Bottled water has evolved into a major industry—moving from a product of necessity to a trendy, luxury product. Is bottled water safer for you than tap water from your faucet? According to the Environmental Protection Agency (EPA), not necessarily. The EPA sets the standards for tap water, and the Food and Drug Administration sets the standards for bottled water based on the EPA's tap water standards. Both kinds are safe if they meet the standards.

drought, try to drink the water before this date. Unopened bottled water doesn't spoil, but the taste can change. If not properly stored in a dark, dry, cool place away from sunlight, household cleaners, and other chemicals, the plastic of the bottle can affect how the water tastes.

You don't have to buy the water you save for a drought emergency. You can bottle your own drinking water—right from your tap. It's best to save drinking water in thoroughly washed, clean plastic bottles, like soda bottles, that have caps you can screw on tightly. However, like store-bought water, your own bottled water should not be kept for more than six months.

Investing in a water purification system may also be of benefit in preparing for a drought. The type you use, such as one that attaches to your faucet or a whole-house water fil-ter, depends on the type of contamination, such as salt, chemicals, or bacteria in your local water supply. Usually, a simple filter attached to your home's incoming water supply will filter out sediment. As a drought drags on, water levels drop. Whether you get water from a city/town water system or from your own well, as the water level falls, impurities

Campers collect and filter water directly from a stream. The best way to prevent consuming any harmful parasites when choosing this method to purify the water is to make sure the filter's pore sizes are less than one micron. When purchasing a filter, make sure there is an active carbon element in the filter.

become concentrated in the water. Common impurities that affect water during a drought are salt and silt. Find out if other impurities may exist in your water from your local county or state health department. Buy a water filter that will filter out these impurities. You'll then be able to safely use the water you have for a longer period of time.

Water also can be purified by boiling or by adding a bit of household bleach. These methods are recommended only for emergencies. It's not for long-term water purification. Suppose that during a drought you find that your water looks or smells strange. For example, your water may look brown and have sediment in it, or it may have an odor. You can first strain it through a clean cloth such as fine-meshed cheesecloth to remove silt and other large particles. Then boil it on the stove. Bring the water to a rolling boil for one full minute. A rolling boil is defined by the top of the water bubbling. Let the water cool before you drink it. Once it's cool, pour it back and forth from one glass to another. This adds oxygen to the water and makes it taste better.

Household bleach may be used in an emergency to purify water you suspect is contaminated. However, only do this with adult permission and supervision. Do not use scented bleach, color-safe bleach, or bleach with cleansers added. You will need to use an eyedropper to add the bleach to the water. Add sixteen drops of regular bleach to one gallon of water. Then stir the water and let it stand for thirty minutes. Smell the water. If it does not smell of bleach, you may add another sixteen drops to the gallon and let it stand for fifteen minutes. If it still does not have a slight bleach odor, it is best to start over with another

☀ Water and Your Health ☀

The human body is made up of about 75 percent water. By drinking up to ten glasses of water a day, the bodily systems, including digestion, metabolism, and absorption, can function properly. Water contains electrolytes, or salts (sodium, potassium, chloride, calcium, magnesium, bicarbonate, phosphate, and sulfate) that are vital to these systems. Electrolytes help cells successfully maintain and transmit impulses within themselves and to other cells. Water is lost from the body through perspiration, urination, and respiration. These processes cannot be stopped, but not replenishing the body with water results in the symptoms of dehydration: excessive thirst, fatigue, headache, dry mouth, dizziness/lightheadedness, infrequent urination, and weakness in the muscles. These are the result of the loss of electrolytes.

gallon of water. The slight bleach smell is a sign that it is safe. Once the water has a slight bleach smell, stir it some more and let it stand until the smell is hardly noticeable. It is then safe to drink.

Water for Other Uses

Remember, too, that you need water for more than drinking. People use water for bathing, cooking, and cleaning. The U.S. government's disaster-relief agency, the Federal Emergency Management Agency (FEMA), recommends that during a drought people have a supply of 1 gallon (3.8 l) of water per day per person to cover all the ways water is used.

Bathing and showering can use a lot of water. During a drought, take very short showers instead of filling up the bathtub for a bath. Taking sponge baths using a bit of warm water in your stoppered bathroom sink uses even less water.

Toilets may be one of the biggest water wasters in the house. This is especially true if you don't have one of the newer low-flush toilets that use no more than 1.6 gallons (6.1 l) of water per flush. (Older toilets use as much as 7 gallons [26.5 l].) You can make your own low-flush toilet. Fill a plastic gallon jug with pebbles or sand. Twist the cap on tightly. Then place the jug inside your toilet tank. The jug takes up room that would otherwise be filled by flushing water.

If you live in a drought-prone area, you might buy or make a rain barrel. Keep it outside where it can collect whatever rain does fall. Or, more specifically, keep it at the side of your house under the gutter to collect rainfall runoff from the roof of your house. You can use this water to keep houseplants alive. You can also use it to water vegetables in a vegetable garden. Using rainwater for watering plants leaves more drinking water for you and your family.

Many types of "used" water can be reused for other purposes. During a drought, it's smart to think of ways you can reuse water instead of pouring it down the drain. Suppose you poured yourself a full glass of water to drink but only drank half a glass. Save the water you didn't drink and use it for something else. Water you use for rinsing dishes may sometimes be used to water plants or to wash the car. Keep a container or jug near the sink and pour used water into it for use later.

Washing clothes in the sink may also save water if you have a water-guzzling washing machine.

Rain barrels provide a great solution for conserving water supplies in cities, where demand for water often exceeds supply. By collecting rainwater to water your garden or lawn and for other household uses, you can save money and be prepared for drought and heat waves. Also, you will be taking part in a practice that has its origins in ancient times. Many households throughout history have collected water this way.

Things to Do Before and During a Drought

Often, a severe drought cannot be prevented. As you've already learned, a drought is part of an area's natural climate cycle. Yet the effects of a drought can be reduced if you use water wisely. If you get used to conserving water in your everyday life, it will be easier for you and your family to get through a drought with less trouble than if you are not used to taking such measures.

There are many things you can do to conserve the water you use both inside and outside your house. Here are just a few.

In general:

- Attach aerators or flow restrictors to all your home's water faucets to reduce the flow of water.

- Repair all dripping faucets. A faucet that drips once per second wastes 2,700 gallons (10,220 l) of water per year! Check faucets and other plumbing often for drips and leaks.

- Buy water-saving, energy-efficient appliances, such as dishwashers and clothes washers. Look for the EnergyGuide on the label of the appliance.

In the bathroom:

- Use a low-flush toilet that uses very little water.

- Do not take baths. Take short showers instead. Baths use a lot more water (about 20 gallons [76 l]) than showers (about 14 gallons [53 l]).

In a short time, leaky faucets can waste gallons of water. Promptly repair any leaky faucets in your home. You can easily find many instructions and tips for this type of repair on the Internet. That way, your household will not have to call a plumber.

- Use an ultra-low-flow showerhead that uses far less water than regular showerheads.

- Never leave the water running while you brush your teeth. Wet your toothbrush, turn the water off, and then turn it on again only when you need to rinse.

- Place a bucket in the bathtub when you take a shower and use it to catch extra water that flows from the showerhead; use this water for other things.

In the kitchen:

- Use a water-saving dishwasher. Run the dishwasher only when it is full, not when it's half empty.

- Use two trays to hand-wash dishes. Use one with soapy water, and the other with rinse water. Then you don't have to keep the water running when you wash and rinse the dishes.

- Save "extra" running water. If it takes a while for the water coming from your faucet to get hot, capture the cooler water in a container and save it to use for something else, like watering plants.

- Do the same for cold water. If it takes a while for your tap water to run cold, save the too-warm water for other uses. For example, collect it in a bottle or pitcher and place it in the refrigerator in order to have cold drinking water.

- Start a compost pile for vegetable waste instead of putting it down the garbage disposal. These devices need lots of water to work properly.

In the laundry room:

- Use a water-saving clothes washer, if possible.

- Use your clothes washer only when you have enough for a full load.

Outdoors and in the garden:

- Plant only native or drought-tolerant plants in your garden. Once they are growing well, these kinds of plants generally do not need to be watered to stay alive.

- Use drip irrigation in your garden to apply water directly to plant roots. This reduces evaporation and saves water, while keeping your plants healthy.

- Use mulch on your garden to hold moisture in the soil.

- Keep your grass lawn 3 inches (7.6 cm) tall. This allows grass to grow deeper roots, which retain moisture.

You can build a compost pile directly on the ground in your backyard. Be sure to build it away from your house. Bugs contribute to the decomposition process, but you don't want them getting inside your house. Your compost is ready when all the organic materials and waste look like rich, dark soil. This process can take from six weeks to two years.

- Avoid using lawn sprinklers, which waste more water than ever reaches the plants' roots. If you must water, do it in a few short sessions and apply the water close to the roots.

Your car:

- Wash your car with your saved water for nondrinking purposes or take it to a professional car wash. Most recycle the water they use.

If your area experiences a severe drought, make sure you follow all the rules and guidelines set by your local or state government to save water. These rules, instituted for

This is one example of the many ways drip irrigation is used today. The drip tubes can be placed in the ground or above the ground. This irrigation system is located in China and is helping to keep a forest fertile during desert conditions. Drip irrigation is a common practice where water is scarce or expensive to access.

the specific drought predicted for your area, will be sent out by mail to all residents and/or communicated by your local TV stations and newspapers. These rules are not intended to make your life difficult. They are intended to make sure that you and your neighbors do not run out of water completely.

Learn that you should never waste water. It's precious. Your life depends on it!

Other Impacts of Drought

Drought affects more than the amount of water you use at home. Severe drought has other, often serious, consequences.

During a drought, plants die or wither. The land becomes parched. Under these conditions, fires can easily be started by lightning or careless people. If there's a drought in your area, avoid making campfires. Be extra careful when you barbecue. And don't ever throw lighted matches or cigarettes or cigars on the ground. The smallest spark can start an enormous, raging fire that may burn many miles of forest, grassland, or even whole towns. To make matters worse, there may not be enough water available to put out fires. So be smart—don't do anything that might spark a fire.

One of the most recent examples of a devastating wildfire that was caused by human carelessness combined with environmental conditions that happened in June 2002. A forestry service employee set papers ablaze. The fire went on to scorch more than 100,000 acres (40,469 ha) of Pike National Forest in Trumbull, Colorado. The combined heat, low humidity, and dryness made the fire hard to contain.

Drought may affect food-growing regions of the country. Certain types of foods may be unavailable. If this happens, talk to your doctor about alternative foods you can eat to stay healthy or about vitamins you can take to get the nutrients you need. It's also a good idea to avoid salty foods during a drought. Salt takes water out of your body, so you become thirsty more often and must drink more water.

Finally, drought may affect electricity generation. Hydroelectric power plants, especially, need abundant water to generate electricity. Other types of power plants, even coal-burning power plants, use water during some part of the process in generating electricity as well. Limit the amount of electricity you use during a drought.

3 --- Heat Waves

As with droughts, the climate conditions that cause heat waves are complicated. They involve many factors that must come together for a heat wave to develop. Unlike a drought, though, most heat waves are relatively short-lived. Most last a week or less, though some may drag on for a month or more. Because North America has seasons, no heat wave will ever last as long as an extended drought. Although heat waves may be short-lived, they can be extremely deadly.

What conditions lead to heat waves? Weather forecasters look for high air pressure and warm air masses in the upper atmosphere during the summer. These conditions may produce a ridge of blocking air in the upper levels of the atmosphere. The blocking ridge forces winds in the upper atmosphere to flow in a clockwise direction. These winds may intensify and form a "dome" of high pressure. The dome traps hazy, humid air near the ground beneath it. As days pass, the surface temperature below the high-pressure air mass rises steadily. The air trapped beneath the blocking ridge holds lots of moisture (humidity) and heats to above-average temperatures.

Geography also plays a part in the development of a heat wave. For example, as air flows down a slope, such as a mountainside, the air mass becomes compressed. (Air pressure is higher at Earth's surface than on mountaintops.) The compressed air may increase the temperature at the surface, causing a heat wave. Weather forecasters call this downsloping, and in summer, heat waves often follow quickly on the heels of winds that flow down toward the surface from higher elevations. The Northeast, for example, may experience a heat wave when air flowing from west to east flows down the eastern slopes of the Appalachian Mountains.

Heat Islands

A heat wave is dangerous in any place under any circumstances. But heat waves become even more deadly when they occur in cities. In summer, cities become urban heat islands. Urban heat islands are between six degrees and eight degrees hotter than surrounding noncity regions. Urban heat islands result from the physical makeup of the city. They are caused by dark-colored paved roads, which

California Heat Waves and Forest Fires

In California, coastal heat waves are often caused by hot, desert air blowing east to west. These winds blow from the scorching Sacramento and San Joaquin valleys toward the coast, which is normally cooled by Pacific Ocean breezes. The hot, dry winds from the interior of the state cause "fire weather." The blustery, hot winds suck nearly all the moisture from the forests. The forests become tinder dry and catch fire easily, especially during lightning storms. Destructive forest fires happen frequently out west in summer. They are major heat wave hazards.

The skyscrapers of New York City are barely visible behind the haze in this photograph taken while the city was under a heat advisory. The scarcity of trees, the absorption of heat into the concrete and asphalt, and the industrial and human activity make many cities several degrees warmer than their surrounding areas. Each city's heat island effect varies based on the particular structures and location of trees in that city. Several steps can be taken to combat the heat island effect. These include planting more trees and constructing roofs and buildings with light-reflective surfaces.

absorb heat. The buildings crowded closely together limit air circulation. There is very little vegetation, which would otherwise provide shade and would cool the air. Air pollution plays an important role in the heat island effect. Air pollution comes from cars and trucks, and especially from power plants. In summer, power plants work at maximum capacity because so many people are using air conditioners, which require more energy to run. A blanket of pollution forms over the baking city. It traps hot air near the sizzling surface and generally prevents cooler air from moving in.

People everywhere may become sick or even die during a severe heat wave. However, the heat island effect causes most deaths and the most severe illnesses in cities during heat waves.

Extreme Heat and What to Do About It

Extreme heat—a heat wave—occurs when an area's temperature is 10° or more above the average high temperature for a relatively prolonged period of time for that area. The high temperatures are often accompanied by high humidity. Humidity not only makes the heat feel worse, but it makes the situation far more dangerous to your health.

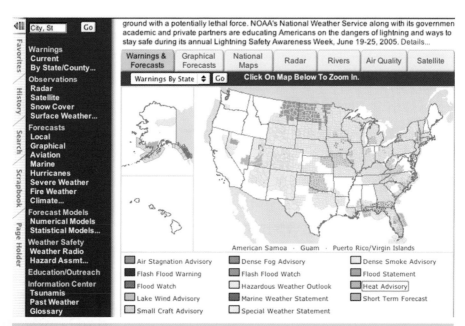

This screen shot from the National Weather Service Web site (http://www.nws.noaa.gov) shows the weather patterns of the United States. On this particular summer day, there are no drought or heat wave warnings, only a heat advisory for parts of Illinois and Missouri. You can visit this Web site to find out information on your city or town and plan your activities accordingly.

Heat waves may occur in any region of the country. You may first hear about a developing heat wave when the local TV weather forecaster cautions of a heat advisory, issued by the National Weather Service (NWS). A heat advisory is issued when heat, with or without high humidity, is expected to develop and may be an inconvenience or a problem for some people. The NWS issues an excessive heat warning when heat, with or without high humidity, is expected to be dangerous for a large proportion of the population.

Why Heat Kills

Extreme heat pushes the body beyond its limits. Warm-blooded creatures (humans) regulate their internal body temperature. Under normal conditions, the body is able to maintain its regular body temperature (98.6°F [37°C]). Even in mildly hot weather, your body produces sweat, which cools your skin as it evaporates. Sweating helps lower your body temperature to normal. Extreme heat and humidity slow down evaporation of sweat from your skin. Your body must then work harder to maintain its normal temperature.

Extreme heat results in the collapse of the body's ability to shed excess heat. When it's really hot, your heart pumps more blood to blood vessels. The blood vessels expand to handle the increased blood flow. More blood is channeled to the tiny blood vessels, called capillaries, near the surface of your skin. This is intended to allow the blood to cool off, assuming that the outside temperature is lower than 98.6°F (37°C). When the outside temperature is higher, the blood cannot cool. It may actually heat up. Further, high humidity prevents the increased sweat from evaporating from your skin and cooling it. Sweating during a heat wave may not cool you off. Instead it may endanger your health as your body loses large amounts of water through your sweat glands, causing dehydration.

The Heat Index

The heat index is the temperature your body actually feels based on the air temperature and humidity. For example, if

Heat Index

About 237 Americans succumb to the taxing demands of heat every year*. Our bodies dissipate heat by varying the rate and depth of blood circulation, by losing water through the skin and sweat glands, and as a last resort, by panting, when blood is heated above 98.6°F. Sweating cools the body through evaporation. However, high relative humidity retards evaporation, robbing the body of its ability to cool itself.

When heat gain exceeds the level the body can remove, body temperature begins to rise, and heat related illnesses and disorders may develop.

The **Heat Index** (HI) is the temperature the body feels when heat and humidity are combined. The chart below shows the HI that corresponds to the actual air temperature and relative humidity. (This chart is based upon shady, light wind conditions. **Exposure to direct sunlight can increase the HI by up to 15°F.)**

(Due to the nature of the heat index calculation, the values in the tables below have an error +/- 1.3F.)

Temperature (F) versus Relative Humidity (%)

°F	90%	80%	70%	60%	50%	40%
80	85	84	82	81	80	79
85	101	96	92	90	86	84
90	121	113	105	99	94	90
95		133	122	113	105	98
100			142	129	118	109
105				148	133	121
110						135

This screenshot of the National Weather Service Web site shows an explanation of the heat index along with a heat index chart (http://www.crh.noaa.gov/pub/heat.php). For example, if your local forecast calls for temperatures to be 100°F (38°C) with 60 percent humidity, according to this chart it will feel like 129°F (53.9°C)! It is important to be aware of the heat index and plan your activities accordingly.

it is 90°F (32°C) outside and the humidity is 80 percent, it feels like it's 113°F (45°C). It is important to note that if you are in direct sunlight during a heat wave, you must add 15° to the heat index to account for the extra heat you get from solar radiation. On the day described above, your body would be experiencing a temperature of 128°F (53°C)!

Heat and Health

If you look at the chart below, you can see the potential health risks as the temperature rises. The hotter it gets based on the heat index chart, the more serious the health effects are.

For example, if the heat index is:

80–90°F 26.7–32.2°C	Fatigue is likely with long exposure to heat or the sun's rays or during outdoor activity.
90–100°F 32.22–38°C	Heatstroke (sunstroke), heat cramps, and heat exhaustion are possible.
105–130°F 40.6–54.4°C	Heatstroke, heat cramps, and heat exhaustion are likely.
130° or greater 54.4°C	Heatstroke is highly likely.

The table on the facing page tells you what each danger is, the symptoms to look for, and what first aid is necessary for each condition.

Heat Disorder	Symptoms	First Aid
Sunburn	Redness and pain. In severe cases, swelling of skin, blisters, fever, headaches.	Ointment for mild cases if blisters appear. If breaking occurs, apply dry sterile dressing. Serious, extensive cases should be seen by a doctor.
Heat Cramps	Painful spasms usually in the muscles of the legs and abdomen. Heavy sweating.	Firm pressure on cramping muscles, or gentle massage to relieve cramping. Give sips of water, as cramping is caused by loss of water and salt imbalance. If nausea occurs, stop giving water.
Heat Exhaustion	Heavy sweating, weakness, cold skin that is pale and clammy. Pulse weak, maybe irregular. Fainting and vomiting (normal body temperature is possible).	Get out of the sun. Lay down and loosen clothes. Apply cool, wet cloths, and fan victim or move to an air-conditioned room. Give sips of water, but stop if it causes nausea. If vomiting continues, go to the emergency room or see a doctor immediately.
Heat Stroke (Sunstroke)	High body temperature (106°F or higher). Hot, red, dry skin. Rapid, strong pulse. Possible loss of consciousness.	HEAT STROKE IS A SEVERE MEDICAL EMERGENCY. GET MEDICAL AID OR GET VICTIM TO A HOSPITAL AT ONCE. DELAY CAN BE FATAL. Move the victim to a cooler environment. Reduce body temperature with a cold bath or sponging. Use extreme caution. Remove clothing, use fans and air conditioners. If temperature rises again, repeat this process. DO NOT GIVE FLUIDS.

4 --- Preparing for and Living with Heat Waves

There are many things you can do to help yourself and your family prepare for a heat wave. One of the most important preparations is to find out where your local community sets up air-conditioned relief centers in case of a health emergency. Your local health department should be able to give you this information. You should keep this information handy—on the refrigerator door or on a family bulletin board. Also, it's a good idea to contact your local Red Cross office to find out what services it offers during a severe heat wave. Keep this phone number with your other emergency phone numbers.

If you can, you should keep an air conditioner or a fan in your home to help you cool off. Remember, however, blackouts frequently occur during heat waves because so many people are using air conditioners.

If your area does not have an official relief center, make a list of places you can go to cool off, even for a little while. You can go to the movies, to the mall or a store, to the library, or to any other public place that might be air-conditioned. Plan to spend the hottest part of the day (during daylight hours) in an air-conditioned place. Some people go to area pools or to the beach during a heat wave. Swimming in cool water is a good way to cool off. Stay out of the sun, as the sun's rays can be very dangerous during a heat wave.

Cooling off in a pool is one way to beat the heat. This young girl is surfacing for air while taking a swim in Alamogordo, New Mexico, where temperatures were creeping toward 100°F (38°C) in June 2005. It is important to remain aware of the dangers of high humidity and direct sunlight while swimming. Be sure to take plenty of rests in the shade and wear sunscreen.

Here's a list of other things you can do to be ready in case of a heat wave.

In your house or apartment:

- Have insulated or heavy blinds or shades on windows (especially south- and west-facing windows that get a lot of direct sun) to keep direct sunlight from heating your house or apartment further.

- Make sure your entire house or apartment and your air conditioner are well sealed and properly insulated. This makes cooling the house or apartment easier and prevents it from warming too much.

- Keep lots of extra water on hand—at least 1 gallon (3.8 l) per person per day. Your body needs extra water during a heat wave.

- Plan to keep your bathtub partly filled with cold water, which you can splash on your face and body to help you keep cool. However, do not do this if there are small children or pets in your home that might fall in!

Yourself and your family:

- Plan to wear light-colored and lightweight summer clothing; light-colored clothing reflects heat and keeps you cooler than heat-absorbing dark-colored clothes.

This young woman is escaping the heat by spending the day at an indoor mall. She is wearing light, loose-fitting clothing in bright, reflective colors. Her hat will protect her head and face from the sun's rays when she has to go back outside.

- Make a plan to change your physical activities if a heat wave strikes. If you are used to jogging outside for an hour every day, it is important to refrain from this during a heat wave. Do not exercise strenuously, only moderately, if necessary. Never exercise outdoors in the heat of the day.

- Make a plan to know what to do if you or

someone in your family has a medical condition, such as heart disease, or is taking medicine that may reduce his or her blood circulation or ability to tolerate heat. Either talk to the family member's doctor about what he or she should do during a heat wave or make sure that the family member has gathered this information for you. Keep this information near your emergency phone numbers.

- Be a good neighbor! Plan to check on your neighbors to see if they are all right during a heat wave. Children and elderly people are less able to regulate extremes of temperature, and so they are at higher risk of dying during a heat wave. Knock on your neighbors' doors to see if they need help.

- Know the signs of heat-related disorders (described earlier) and what to do. Keep emergency phone numbers handy.

During a Heat Wave: Things to Do and Not to Do

Slow down! Do not do strenuous activity—especially during the heat of the day. Instead, take it easy—relax. Stay in cool or shady places. If you must do some physical activity, do it during the coolest part of the day, usually between 4:00 AM and 7:00 AM.

Do not stay in the sun! Sunburn slows down your skin's ability to cool itself. The sun will also heat the inside of your body. This makes you sweat more. You'll lose more water, and it will be harder for your body to maintain its internal temperature. If you must be out in the sun, use a strong sunscreen (SPF 15 or higher).

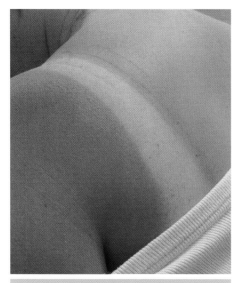

Sunburn limits your body's ability to cope with heat during a heat wave. Effects of exposure can range from slight tenderness to blisters to acute sunburn.

Stay indoors as much as possible. If you don't have air-conditioning, try to stay on a lower floor of a building. Hot air rises, so lower floors are cooler.

Close all window shades, blinds, and curtains to keep the sun and heat out of your home. If you don't have air-conditioning or a fan, keep all windows open from the bottom to allow air to circulate. Open windows more at night, so cool

The Number One Killer

In the United States, heat waves cause more total deaths than any other natural hazard—more than tornadoes, hurricanes, floods, or earthquakes. About 175 Americans die during heat waves every year. Between 1936 and 1975, about 20,000 people in the United States died from the effects of heat and intense solar radiation. In the terrible heat wave of 1980 alone, more than 1,250 people died. These deaths represent victims directly affected by the heat wave. It is estimated that thousands more die of heat waves' indirect effects, such as heart attack and worsening of disease as the body weakens.

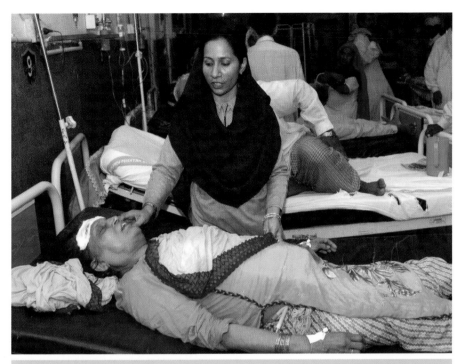

A nurse attends to a victim of heatstroke at a hospital in Multan, Pakistan, on June 24, 2005. Temperatures rose to 122°F (50°C), causing hundreds of people to be hospitalized for dehydration and heatstroke. There are two types of heatstroke: exertional heat stroke, which usually affects young people engaged in strenuous exercise in a hot environment, and classic nonexertional heat stroke, which often affects elderly people during a heat wave.

air can enter your home. However, in case these windows are on an upper floor of your house or apartment and there are small children and/or pets present, do not open from the bottom unless you have window guards or can otherwise secure the safety of the children and pets.

Wear loose-fitting, light-colored clothing to reflect the sun's heat. Wear a wide-brimmed hat to keep the sun off your head and avoid sunstroke.

Closing blinds and curtains to the sunlight can help keep you cool during the day. During a heat wave, it is vital to your health to take refuge in shaded, cool areas away from sunlight.

Drink lots of water. Even if you don't feel thirsty, your body may need water. If your body dehydrates—loses lots of water—you can get very sick or even die.

Do not drink beverages that have caffeine (coffee, tea, caffeinated colas) or alcohol (especially beer). These drinks make heat's effects on your body even worse and tend to dehydrate your body.

Do not eat salty foods, as they take vital water out of your body's cells. Eat frequent, smaller meals, which your body does not have to use a lot of energy to digest all at once (digestion raises your body temperature).

Children or pets should never be left alone in a closed car. The temperature inside a closed car with its windows up can rise to over 140°F (60°C) in minutes—and such high temperatures can kill within minutes. If the driver can't take the child or pet with him or her if he or she leaves the car, it is best for the child or pet to be left in the care of a trusted person at home.

Here are examples of food and drinks to avoid during a heat wave. Caffeinated drinks, such as colas, lead to dehydration. During a heat wave, it is important to be able to sweat. These types of drinks hinder that process. Water is safest to drink, but natural fruit juices and sports beverages can replace salts lost from sweating. Salty foods, such as chips, affect your body's ability to sweat properly.

Heat waves are very often associated with droughts. Even if the drought accompanying the heat wave is a short-term water shortage, conserving water during a heat wave is smart. Keep extra water on hand, but use it wisely.

5 --- The Heat Is On!

In the summer of 2003, Europe experienced an intense heat wave that left 35,000 people dead. Scientists from around the world say that killer heat waves and droughts are likely to become more common as the world's climate changes.

The world's climate scientists agree that it is human activity that is causing the world climate to change, or specifically to warm up. Global warming is the result of the billions of tons of greenhouse gases released into the atmosphere every year as a result of human activity.

A greenhouse gas is a gas that traps heat near Earth's surface. The process is called the greenhouse effect. The greenhouse effect is not bad—in fact, life on Earth exists because of the greenhouse effect. It was greenhouse gases—water vapor, carbon dioxide, and methane—in Earth's early atmosphere that allowed life to develop. But since the Industrial Revolution of the 1800s, people have been burning fuels that add enormous amounts of carbon dioxide to the air. The fuels that release the most carbon dioxide are called fossil fuels because they come from plants that died many millions of years ago. Burning fossil fuels—oil, natural gas, coal—has put so much extra carbon dioxide in the air that more and more heat is being trapped near Earth's surface and is warming its climate.

☀ Carbon Dioxide Rising ☀

As this graph shows, the level of carbon dioxide in the atmosphere has been increasing year by year. Carbon dioxide is one of the main gases causing global warming. To reduce the amount of carbon dioxide you put into the air, burn as little fossil fuel as possible. Save electricity. Drive fuel-efficient cars. Ride a bike!

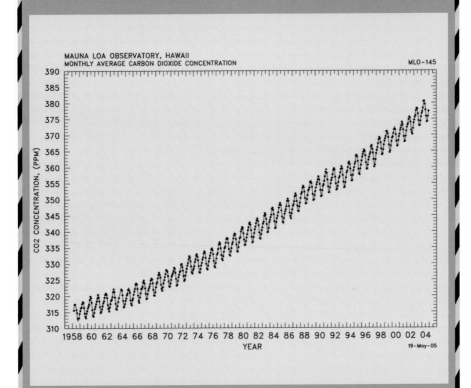

MAUNA LOA OBSERVATORY, HAWAII
MONTHLY AVERAGE CARBON DIOXIDE CONCENTRATION
MLO-145

Mauna Loa, Hawaii, is considered one of the best locations for testing air. This is because human and vegetation influences are minimal, which bring about more accurate results. Testing here began in 1958. The largest jump in CO_2 levels occurred from 1997 to 1998. The concentration is measured in parts per million by volume.

Gas pipelines and storage tanks are pictured here. Some scientist argue that it is important for energy providers to find alternative sources that do not exasperate the greenhouse effect, meaning sources that release the lowest amount of carbon possible.

Of course, the hotter Earth's climate gets, the more heat waves many parts of the planet will suffer. Scientists in England predict that deadly heat waves—like the one in Europe in 2003—will happen twice as often as they did before. Other scientists predict that droughts will be more common, will be more severe, and will last longer. In fact, climate scientists in Colorado have shown that the amount of land parched by drought doubled between 1970 and 2000. The higher temperatures caused by global warming have stripped a huge amount of soil of its moisture, making it useless for growing crops.

Scientists predict that the situation will likely get worse. A 2005 study found that the global temperature may rise by as much as 3.6° to 19.8° by the middle of this century. Such a huge increase would have a dramatic effect on climate and would likely devastate plants, animals, and people.

These studies are based on a doubling of greenhouse gases in the atmosphere over their preindustrial levels 200

One of many results of the 2003 European heat wave is pictured here: a parched lake bed that at one time provided drinking water to three French cities. When such water sources are depleted, it then becomes necessary for other sources to provide water, which can lead to depletion of these secondary sources.

to 250 years ago. If we don't do something to help stop global warming, then heat waves, droughts, and other severe climate events and changes may disrupt not only our lives but every living thing on Earth.

There are some things you can do to help slow down global warming:

- Talk to your parents about driving a car that uses less gasoline. Fuel-efficient cars such as gas-electric hybrids use far less gasoline than SUVs, for example.

- Inform your parents about the importance of insulating your house to save on the amount of heating fuel you use. Insulation will also reduce the amount of electricity you use to run your air conditioner. If you live in an

Many consumers are scrambling to buy fuel-efficient, environmentally friendly hybrid cars, such as the Toyota Prius pictured here. The battery recharges automatically as the car is driven. Driving a fuel-efficient vehicle is perhaps one of the most effective ways a consumer can protect the environment.

apartment, you can bring the importance of this issue to the attention of the building owner or landlord. Within your apartment, you can install weather stripping and caulk holes, cracks, and openings around windows, doors, and walls.

- Save electricity. Most electricity is produced by burning coal, so lowering your electric use is a good way to help reduce global warming.

Did you know that recycling paper products also helps conserve water? According to the EPA, recycling one ton of paper saves seventeen trees and 7,000 gallons (26,500 l) of water. It also produces far less air pollution.

- Recycle paper and paper products. Paper comes from trees, and trees help take carbon dioxide out of the air. Recycling helps save trees and reduces the amount of carbon dioxide in the atmosphere.

- Become an energy crusader! Use as little electricity as possible. Turn off the lights when you leave a room. Don't leave your computer on when you're not using it. If you or your parents are buying something electric, find out if you can buy a product that uses less electricity than other models.

- Do not ask your parents to drive you places. Take a bike or use public transportation. Bikes only burn the fuel in your body, so they keep you fit and don't add carbon dioxide to the air. Public transportation—especially trains—uses far less fuel per person than a car.

Most important, inform yourself. Learn about what is happening to the world climate. Then find out all the things that you can do to help.

Glossary

aerator An apparatus attached to the end of a faucet spout that restricts water flow and mixes air into the flowing water.

agricultural drought A type of seasonal drought that affects the moisture in the soil and, therefore, affects crops.

air pressure How close together or far apart the molecules in the air are; the weight of the air at a given altitude.

arid Dry, as in a dry climate that gets little rain.

blocking high An area of stationary, high-pressure air that blocks the movement of air masses through it.

cell A specific portion of the atmosphere that is behaving as a unit or center of a specific activity.

compost pile A heap of decaying vegetation and other organic matter to be used as fertilizer.

conserve To save or preserve.

dehydration The excessive loss of water from the body of an organism.

devastating drought A drought that is hard to predict or occurs without warning.

downsloping The movement of air flowing down a slope, such as a mountainside.

drip irrigation A water-conserving form of irrigation where water is released in timed drops or small increments directly to the root of plants.

drought A relatively long-lasting reduction in the percentage of normal precipitation a region gets.

excessive heat warning A warning issued when the heat index will reach at least 105°F (40.6°C) for a duration of at least three hours for two consecutive days, or the heat index will reach 115°F (46°C) for any duration of time.

heat advisory Report issued when the heat index is expected to range from 105°F to 115°F (40°C to 46°C) for a duration of at least three hours during the daytime.

heat index An index that combines the temperature and humidity to give a number that tells what the weather feels like in degrees.

heat wave A period of above-normal temperatures over a particular region.

humidity The amount of moisture held in the air.

hydroelectric Using falling or otherwise moving water to drive a generator to produce energy.

hydrological drought A prolonged period of below-normal precipitation resulting in below-normal groundwater and/or lake and reservoir levels.

invisible drought A prolonged period when evaporation exceeds rainfall and water levels drop. There is some precipitation but not enough.

jet stream The strong winds that are concentrated in a narrow stream in the atmosphere. The position of the jet stream affects weather patterns.

meteorological drought A type of drought only defined in terms of the dryness of the climate and/or lack of precipitation compared to the normal amount for the area.

mid-latitudes The latitudes of the temperate zones that fall in the range of 30 to 60 degrees north or south of the equator.

monsoon Seasonal winds that blow over ocean water and bring rain to various regions of the world, such as India.

mulch An organic substance or other loose material spread over soil and around plants to conserve soil moisture.

precipitation Rain, snow, sleet, or hail that falls to the ground from clouds.

recycle To re-form and reuse materials that were used previously for other things and to make them into new things.

seasonal drought A drought occurring in a region that usually gets most of its rain in one season.

silt Particles of sand or rock that can be circulated in air or water.

solar radiation The energy given off by the sun in the form of visible light, heat (infrared), and other forms of electromagnetic radiation.

tinder dry Capable of starting a fire.

westerlies The winds that flow east to west in the mid-latitudes found in both hemispheres.

For More Information

American Red Cross
National Headquarters
2025 E Street NW
Washington, DC 20006
(202) 303-4498
Disaster assistance: (866) 438-4636
Web site: http://www.redcross.org

CARE USA
Headquarters
151 Ellis Street
Atlanta, GA 30303
(404) 681-2552
Web site: http://www.careusa.org

Drought Mitigation Center
University of Nebraska–Lincoln
239 L.W. Chase Hall
P.O. Box 830749
Lincoln, NE 68583-0749
(402) 472-6707
Web site: http://www.drought.unl.edu

Federal Emergency Management Agency (FEMA)
500 C Street SW
Washington, DC 20472
(202) 566-1600
Free publications: (800) 480-2520
Web site: http://www.fema.org

National Weather Service
1325 East West Highway
Silver Spring, MD 20910
Web site: http://www.nws.noaa.gov

Web Sites

Due to the changing nature of Internet links, the Rosen Publishing Group, Inc., has developed an online list of Web sites related to the subject of this book. This site is updated regularly. Please use the link below to access the list:

http://www.rosenlinks.com/lep/drhw

For Further Reading

Bender, Lionel. *Heat and Drought.* Austin, TX: Raintree Publishing, 1998.

Bonnifield, Paul. *The Dust Bowl.* Albuquerque, NM: University of New Mexico Press, 1979.

Challen, Paul C. *Drought and Heat Wave Alert.* New York, NY: Crabtree Publishing, 2004.

Jennings, Terry. *Drought: Investigating Natural Disasters.* London, England: Chrysalis Education, 1999.

Klinenberg, Eric. *Heat Wave: A Social Autopsy of Disaster in Chicago.* Chicago, IL: University of Chicago Press, 2003.

Spilsbury, Louise. *Dreadful Droughts.* Portsmouth, NH: Heinemann Publishing, 2003.

Thomas, Rick. *Sizzle! A Book About Heat Waves.* Minneapolis, MN: Picture Window Books, 2005.

Ylvisaker, Anne. *Droughts.* Monkato, MN: Capstone Books, 2003.

Bibliography

Allaby, Michael. *Droughts*. New York, NY: Facts on File, 1998.

American Red Cross. "Heat Waves." Retrieved May 10, 2005 (http://www.redcross.org/services/disaster/0,1082,0_586_,00.html).

Bhattacharya, Shaoni. "European Heatwave Caused 35,000 Deaths." October 10, 2003. NewScientist.com. Retrieved May 10, 2005 (http://www.newscientist.com/article.ns?id=dn4259&print=true).

Bonnifield, Paul. *The Dust Bowl: Men, Dirt, and Depression*. Albuquerque, NM: University of New Mexico Press, 1979.

Dolan, Edward F. *Drought: The Past, Present, and Future Enemy*. New York, NY: Franklin Watts, 1990.

Eilperin, Juliet. "Humans May Double the Risk of Heat Waves." *Washington Post*. December 2, 2004. Retrieved May 10, 2005 (http://www.washingtonpost.com/ac2/wp-dyn/A26605-2004Dec1?language=printer).

FEMA. "Are You Ready? Extreme Heat." Retrieved May 10, 2005 (http://www.fema.gov/areyouready/heat/hazards/extremeheat/heat.shtm).

Heat Island Group. "High Temperatures." Retrieved May 10, 2005 (http://eetd.lbl.gov/HeatIsland/HighTemps).

Heat Is Online. "Scientists Predict Rising Global Temperature Range." Retrieved May 17, 2005 (http://www.heatisonline.org/contentserver/objecthandlers/index.cfm?id=5072&method=full).

National Center for Atmospheric Research & the UCAR Office of Programs. "Drought's Growing Reach: NCAR Study Points to Global Warming as Key Factor." January 10, 2005. Retrieved May 10, 2005 (http://www.ucar.edu/news/releases/2005/drought_research.shtml).

National Drought Mitigation Center. "Mitigating Drought." Retrieved May 10, 2005 (http://drought.unl.edu/mitigate/mitigate.htm).

National Drought Mitigation Center. "Monitoring Drought." Retrieved May 10, 2005 (http://drought.unl.edu/monitor/monitor.htm).

National Drought Mitigation Center. "Planning for Drought." Retrieved May 10, 2005 (http://drought.unl.edu/plan/plan.htm).

National Drought Mitigation Center. "Understanding Your Risk." Retrieved May 10, 2005 (http://drought.unl.edu/risk/risk.htm).

National Drought Mitigation Center. "What Is Drought?" Retrieved May 10, 2005 (http://drought.unl.edu/whatis/what.htm).

National Weather Service. "Heat Waves." Retrieved May 10, 2005 (http://hprcc.unl.edu/nebraska/heatwave.html).

National Weather Service Forecast Office. "Heat Index." Retrieved May 10, 2005 (http://www.crh.noaa.gov/pub/heat.php).

Planet Ark. "Humans Raise Risk of Europe Heatwaves." Retrieved May 10, 2005 (http://www.planetark.com/avantgo/dailynewsstory.cfm?newsid=28386).

Smith, Howard E., Jr. *Killer Weather: Stories of Great Disasters.* New York, NY: Dodd, Mead & Co., 1982.

The University of Chicago Press. "Dying Alone in the Heatwave: An Interview with Eric Klinenberg." Retrieved May 25, 2005 (http://www.press.uchicago.edu/Misc/Chicago/443213in.html).

The Weather Channel. "Encyclopedia: Heat Wave Advisories and Warnings." Retrieved May 10, 2005 (http://www.weatherclassroom.com/encyclopedia/heat_wave/advisories_and_warnings.php).

Index

About the Author

Natalie Goldstein has been a writer of science books and educational materials for more than fifteen years. She has written extensively in the fields of environmental, earth, and life sciences. Among her books are the *Earth Almanac*, *Rebuilding Prairies and Forests*, *The Nature of the Oceans*, *Viruses,* and *Looking Inside.* She has worked for the Nature Conservancy, the Hudson River Foundation, the World Wildlife Fund, and the Audubon Society. A member of the National Association of Science Writers and the Society of Environmental Journalists, Ms. Goldstein holds master's degrees in environmental science and education.

Photo Credits

Cover, pp. 1, 5, 13, 14, 17, 27, 32, 39, 43, 49, 50 © AP/Wide World Photos; p. 6 © P. Greer/Chicago Tribune/Corbis Sygma; pp. 10, 45 by Tahara Anderson; p. 15 courtesy of the National Oceanic and Atmospheric Administration/ Department of Commerce; p. 18 © Phil Schermeister/ Corbis; p. 22 © Carl and Ann Purcell/ Corbis; p. 24 © Tom Young/Corbis; p. 26 © Sally A. Morgan, Ecoscene/Corbis; p. 28 © Reuters/Corbis; pp. 33, 35 http://www.noaa.gov; p. 40 © Roy Morsch/Zefa/Corbis; p. 42 © Sonda Dawes/The Image Works; p. 44 © Cloud Nine Prod./Zefa/Corbis; p. 47 courtesy of the Carbon Dioxide Information Analysis Center, Oak Ridge National Laboratory, United States Department of Energy; p. 48 © Zuma/Corbis; p. 51 © Tom Stewart/Corbis.

Designer: Tahara Anderson; Editor: Leigh Ann Cobb